Things Girls Love

Story by Jenna Winterberg • Illustrations by Diana Fisher

Walter Foster
Jr.

Meet Dotty. Dotty is a ladybug. Ladybugs, as a rule, are not very adventurous. Dotty likes to fly and flit about here and there, but what she really enjoys is relaxing at her home in the clover patch. In the clover patch, there is always plenty of sunshine—but very little excitement.

Draw Dotty the ladybug!

1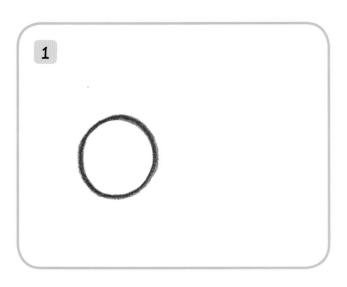

2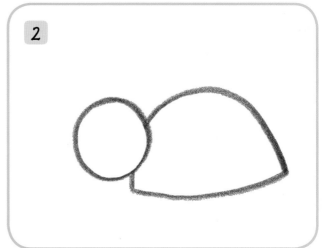

3

4

5

6

When you finish your drawing, place the sun sticker on the opposite page!

Dotty never went looking for adventure, but one day adventure came looking for her! As she relaxed on a clover, a big gust of wind swept her away from her home! The wind lifted her up, up, up—and before she knew it, she was carried high above the apple trees!

Draw the apple tree!

When you finish your drawing, place the apple bucket sticker on the opposite page!

Dotty flapped her wings helplessly as the strong wind that picked her up whooshed her back down! She squeezed her eyes shut as the ground approached. When Dotty finally dared to take a peek, she found herself safely cradled in the center of a large sunflower.

Draw the sunflower!

When you finish your drawing, place the cloud sticker on the opposite page!

Dotty was covered in pollen from the sunflower. As she stood up and began dusting off all the sticky stuff, Dotty saw Buzz the bumble-bee zoom by! The busy bee was hard at work collecting flower pollen to take back to his honeycomb home.

Draw Buzz the bumblebee!

When you finish your drawing, place the beehive sticker on the opposite page!

Dotty shouted and waved wildly to catch Buzz's attention. But he was too focused on his work to notice the lost ladybug. Luckily, Chase the butterfly came fluttering by! Chase listened carefully to Dotty's unusual story. He knew the way to Dotty's clover patch—so he offered to take her there on his back!

Draw Chase the butterfly!

1

2

3

4

5

6

When you finish your drawing, place the caterpillar sticker on the opposite page!

With Dotty on board, Chase took flight. Soon Dotty spotted the clover patch. Delighted, she pointed toward her home—but in her excitement, she let go of Chase! All of a sudden, Dotty tumbled off the butterfly's back. Chase didn't even notice that Dotty had fallen—or that she landed on the back of a turtle!

Draw Sheldon the turtle!

When you finish your drawing, place the butterfly sticker on the opposite page!

The turtle introduced himself as Sheldon. Then he asked the frazzled ladybug how she ended up on his shell. Dotty explained the sticky spot she was in as she fluttered to the ground. Sheldon knew the clover patch, so he offered to show Dotty the way home. Just then, Harriet the bunny came speeding toward them!

Draw Harriet the bunny!

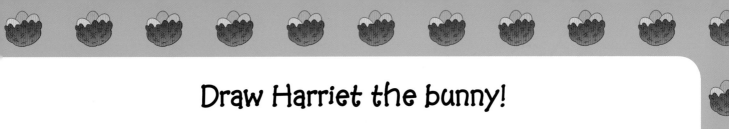

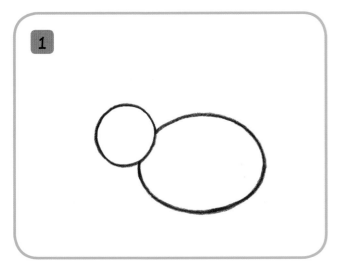 1

 2

 3

 4

 5

 6

When you finish your drawing, place the bird's nest sticker on the opposite page!

Dotty had to think quickly to avoid being run
over by the racing rabbit! The brave little bug
beat her wings with all her might, landing
near a small pond, where she spotted a bright
green bullfrog perched on a lily pad.

Draw Jeremiah the bullfrog!

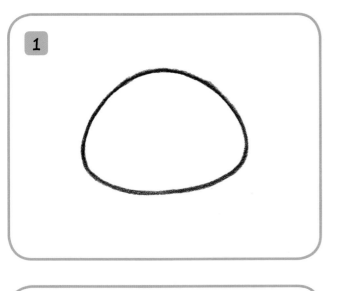

1

2

3

4

5

6

When you finish your drawing, place the dragonfly sticker on the opposite page!

Dotty called out to the frog for help, but it was not the frog that answered! "Jeremiah cannot hear you," a voice said, "but I can." A friendly snail named Cargo had crept up to Dotty's side. Cargo told Dotty that all she had to do to find her clover patch was look for the end of the rainbow!

Draw Cargo the snail!

When you finish your drawing, place the fish sticker on the opposite page!

Dotty thanked Cargo and set out once again to find her clover patch. Just then, a big drop of rain splashed down from the sky. "Rain!" Dotty happily exclaimed, hoping the rain would bring a rainbow. Then she looked up and saw a beautiful unicorn standing below the dazzling rainbow she had wished for!

Draw the unicorn!

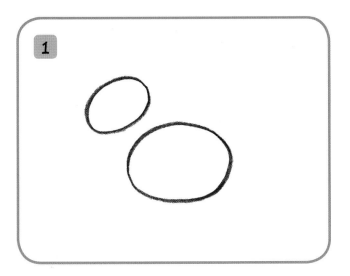

When you finish your drawing, place the pot of gold sticker on the opposite page!

Dotty thought she saw the unicorn wink at her. She blinked her eyes in disbelief, then looked again. The unicorn had disappeared—but the rainbow still gleamed brightly. Dotty followed the rainbow to her clover-patch home. There she crawled onto her favorite four-leaf clover and dreamt about her adventure.

Draw the four-leaf clover!

When you finish your drawing, place the clover sticker on the opposite page!

The end.